Kung Fu Katy
and the Horrors

By Sally-Ann Lever

Illustrated by David Pace

What a gorgeously hot sunny day it was. Kung Fu Katy's mum, Mrs Peep, was driving her old clankety, clankety, bang-bang-banger down the road, while Katy sat in the back with her nose all squashed up against the window, happily watching the world go by. They were on their way to Victoria Station. They were going to collect Katy's twin cousins Hughie and Henry Horror and their mum Aunty Dolly Horror, who were coming all the way from Brighton to stay with Katy and her mother for the weekend.

And how pretty Kung Fu Katy looked, all dressed up for the occasion in a pretty pink dress with daisies dotted all over. She had matching ribbons tied round her bunches, shiny patent shoes, five frilly petticoats under her skirt to make it stand out like a ballerina's tu-tu, a row of pop-together-pearls and one of her mum's old white handbags strapped safely round her shoulder.

"Isn't it a shame that we've never had a chance to meet our cousins, the Horrors, before," said Mrs Peep. "I was so thrilled to receive that letter from Aunty Dolly last week, saying how she and the boys would like to visit us after all these years, that I could hardly wait to reply."

"Oooo yes," said Katy, "I bet we're going to have the best weekend ever!"

"And I want you to behave like a lady," said Mrs Peep. "None of that funny yelling and jumping around stuff you do from time to time. It really isn't a nice way for a little girl to behave, you know."

But Katy wasn't listening. She was so excited. What fun it was going to be, having two little boys stay in her house for two whole days and nights.

She gazed out of the window.
She watched the leaves on the trees blow in the breeze.
She watched the birds in the sky flutter and fly.
She watched the huffs and puffs of mucky grey smoke, popping and coughing out of the wobbly old exhaust.
"Chugg-Chugg ... pop! pop! ... Chugg-Chugg ... pop! pop! ..."

"Oh dear," sighed Mrs Peep. "I do wish this old car would go a little faster. That train from Brighton arrives in six and a half minutes and I would hate to be late to collect the Horrors."

Then all of a sudden, oh dear me, all of a horrible sudden, the old car skidded and wheezed to a halt.

It skidded and wheezed and sneezed and popped and smoked and choked and suddenly stopped - BANG! right in the middle of the road.

"OH NO!" cried Mrs Peep. "That's done it! We'll never get to the station on time now."

"Don't worry Mum," said Kung Fu Katy, leaping out of the car. "Let's try and find out what the trouble is."

Mrs Peep followed Katy out of the car and helped lift the creaky bonnet.

Katy stared at the tangled engine and scratched her head.

"No problem, Mummy," she said. "I can fix it. You check
under the car, while I fiddle around here."

"Now don't you go and get yourself dirty dear,"
said Mrs Peep. "It would be such a shame to spoil that
lovely new dress."

"Don't worry, Mum," said Katy. "I won't."

So Mrs Peep walked to the back of the car, bent down and
disappeared right underneath.

Then Kung Fu Katy got to work.

She stood very, very, very still. She breathed in very, very, very deeply. Then all of a sudden she kicked off her shoes, and as quick as two flickers she yanked up her sleeves, stuffed her skirt in her knickers, she flexed up her muscles and with a MIGHTY big blow she belted the engine and yelled out, "YAAAAAAASOOOOOOWWWWWWWW!!" and BANG! BLAST! CHOP! CHOP! CHOP! Kung Fu Katy couldn't stop.

She clouted the engine with her left hand, WHAM!!

She clobbered the engine with her right hand, SLAM !!

And would you believe it, that little old car jumped and
wriggled and puffed and giggled and in two seconds flat
began breathing like a brand new baby.

"It's working, Mum! It's working!" cried Kung Fu Katy,
pulling out her petticoats and puffing up her sleeves.

"Quick! Get back in the car! Get back in the car!"

Mrs Peep popped her head out from under the car.

"Did you hear that funny noise?" she said.

"What funny noise?" said Kung Fu Katy.

"A great yelling noise," said Mrs Peep, "like somebody with
a terrible tummy ache."

"No," said Katy, "I never heard a thing."

"Oh well, it must have been that rusty old engine," said Mrs Peep. "Still, you're a very clever girl to have got it started like that. I shall never know how you did it."

Katy smiled. She did most of her kung fu tricks when her mum wasn't looking because Mrs Peep thought it absolutely awful for a little girl to behave like some hooligan heavy-weight boxer.

Still, they jumped back in the car, slammed the doors and zoomed off at top speed to Victoria Station.

Well, they arrived just in time.

Just in time to park the car, push through the crowds and see the 13.20 train from Brighton make its way into platform two.

Katy and her mummy were so excited they could hardly hide it! They watched and waved and whistled and jumped and hopped and skipped and bopped and bounced, and as the noisy rumpus faded away, there, in a great messy huddle, in the middle of the platform, stood their cousins, the Horrors.

And, oh dear me, what a bunch they were.

Aunty Dolly looked like a fancy Christmas cake.
She jingled in jangly jewellery. She wore a hairy tickly
coat, and her yellow curly hair was piled high on top of
her head like a huge scrambled egg.

As for the two boys, Henry and Hughie, well, they looked
the messiest, dirtiest, scruffiest, filthiest two little boys
that you've ever seen in all your life.

BRIGHTON 2

NO
ENTRY

Hughie wore a red and green checked suit with all his breakfast stuck, stained and dried down his middle. And Henry - Henry wore exactly the same suit as Hughie, but with all his buttons done up the wrong way round and a dirty sock hanging out of his pocket which he used to wipe his runny nose.

They looked shocking.

Aunty Dolly pulled a long white hanky out of her handbag and waved it in the air. "Yooo-hooooo!" she called, "Yoooooo-hoooooo! We're here! We're here!"

The two boys didn't waste a second. They charged down the platform like a couple of roaring bulls, bashing into people smashing into trolleys and knocking everybody's things all over the place. They screeched to a crashing halt just in front of Kung Fu Katy and her mum.

"WE'RE THE HORRORS!" boomed Hughie proudly.

"Yes, we can see that," said Mrs Peep.

"And we need a crane," said Henry.

"A crane?" said Mrs Peep.

"Yes, a crane," said Hughie.

"To lift me mum's cases out of the train," said Henry. "She's bought ten of them, each one jam-packed and stuffed to the top with all her rubbish."

"We got a crane to put them on the train," said Hughie.

"But now we need another crane to take them off the train again," said Henry.

"Oh, that's a shame," said Mrs Peep.

"I'll do it!" said Katy.

"You do it?" barked Hughie. "HAH!"

"You do it?" laughed Henry. "HAH! You could never do it. Not in a hundred million years. You're just a stupid girl, in a soppy dress and you couldn't lift one of these cases, not even if you tried."

Katy looked at Hughie. Katy looked at Henry. Katy looked at her mum.

"Look up there," she said.

"Where?" they said.

"Up there behind you," she said.

As they turned round and looked up, Katy kicked off her shoes, and as quick as two flickers, she yanked up her sleeves, stuffed her skirt in her knickers, flexed her muscles and with a MIGHTY big blow she leapt off the ground and yelled out, "YAAAAAAAASSOOWWWWWWWW!!" and BANG! BLAST! CHOP! CHOP! CHOP! Kung Fu Katy couldn't stop.

Her darting legs pounded the air like a pair of whizzing rockets,

woooooooooooooooooooooooooooooooooooooooooooooooooshhh.

Her tiny feet spun round faster than a pair of
propelling helicopter blades,
swoooooooooooooooooooooooooooooooooooooooooooooooshhhh.
Then she kicked the carriage door with such an
incredible sock – WHAAAAAAM!
that would you believe it, Aunty Dolly's huge heavy cases
shuddered and shook, flew out of the window and landed
right on top of a passing trolley, each one on top of the
other, stacked in a perfect pile.

"Where to, Miss?" said the friendly porter pushing the
wobbly trolley.

"Follow me," said Katy, puffing up her petticoats and
slipping back into her patent shoes.

"Oh my, my, my," said Aunty Dolly. "What a clever little girl
you are. And what a lot of trouble you saved me. Come over
here and give us a kiss!"

Katy smiled. Even though Aunty Dolly looked a bit silly in
that soppy coat and hair-do, she really seemed very nice.
So Katy skipped over to her aunty and gave her a great
big welcoming hug hello.

Hughie and Henry turned their heads and looked around.

"HEY! Who did that?" yelled Hughie.

"Who put all those cases on to the trolley
like that?"

"Katy did," said Aunty Dolly. "All by herself
and without even lifting a finger. If you
hadn't been so busy
looking up at the
ceiling you would have
seen for yourself."

"Oh don't be potty, Mum!" said Hughie.

"Oh don't be dotty, Mum!" said Henry. "She's a girl. A girl could never have done a thing like that."

And the two boys roared and laughed and followed Katy back to the car with Mrs Peep and Aunty Dolly and the friendly porter with the wobbly trolley, trailing just behind.

Anyway, the friendly porter very kindly helped strap Aunty Dolly's huge heavy cases on to the roof of the car. Everybody squeezed in, and Mrs Peep began the drive back home.

The two mums were so delighted to see each other that they didn't stop chattering and talking, while Kung Fu Katy sat squashed in between the two Horrors, who didn't stop screeching and squawking.

Poor Katy. How bitterly sad and disappointed she felt. She had been so looking forward to meeting her two new cousins and how horribly nasty and rude they had both turned out to be.

Henry blew his nose into his sock and made a revolting raspberry sound ... Thbbrrrrrrr.

Hughie pulled a long pink line of bubble-gum out from his mouth and stuck the end of it on to Katy's cheek. "Relatives should stick together!" he shrieked.

The two boys rumbled and roared and giggled all the way back home.

They were just awful.

As soon as they arrived in the drive of the Peeps' pretty home, Mrs Peep dashed into the kitchen, put the kettle on and made a hot pot of tea and the most delicious plate of yummy sandwiches, biscuits and cakes you've ever seen. Katy showed Aunty Dolly to the toilet.

The twins jumped up and down on the sofa and rolled all over the floor.

Then they all sat down at the table and Katy poured the tea.

"Oooooooooo, what a delicious spread," said Aunty Dolly tucking her napkin under her chin. "Would you mind if I helped myself?"

"Not at all," said Mrs Peep. "Please tuck in and enjoy yourself."

"I'll serve you, Aunty Dolly," said Kung Fu Katy. "What would you like?"

"Oh, how kind," said Aunty Dolly gratefully. "Thanks ever so much. Now let's see ... I think I'll have a peanut butter sandwich, a custard cream, a coffee eclair and a warm sticky doughnut."

"Here you are then," said Katy, having piled up all the delicious goodies on to a plate. "Enjoy your tea."

"HEY! What about us?" yelled Hughie.

"YEAH! We're absolutely starving!" shouted Henry.

"So give us everything that's left on the table and all the crumbs too."

"Okey dokey," said Kung Fu Katy. "You asked for it, and here it comes."

With that, she leapt off her chair, jumped in the air, and yelling "EEEEEEEE-YOWWWWWWWW!!!" she smashed her feet right down on to the tea table with such an ENORMOUS thud, that all the food shot off the plates, swooshed through the air and sploshed and plopped all over Hughie and Henry Horror's heads.

SPLAT!

SPLODGE!

Plop.

Plop.   Plop.

Mrs Peep looked furious.

Aunty Dolly looked somewhat curious.

And Hughie and Henry were so shocked, they could hardly
believe their horrible little eyes.

"COR!! How did you ever do that then?" gasped Henry.

"It's probably a trick she learnt off the Paul Daniels show," said Hughie.

"Actually, it's kung fu," said Katy.

"Kung who?" said Henry.

"Kung fu," said Katy.

"Well, it wasn't very ladylike whatever it was," said Mrs Peep crossly. "Fancy jumping on the tea table like that, Katy. You really are a naughty girl."

"Sorry, Mum," said Katy. "I was only practising my martial arts."

"Never mind about all that," said Mrs Peep. "You children had better run off into the garden to play. It'll give Aunty Dolly and me a chance to clear up all this mess and have a good old chatter and gossip."

"Grrrreat!" cried Kung Fu Katy. "Come on boys, follow me."

"But remember one thing," warned Mrs Peep. "There's a hole in the fence at the bottom of the garden. It's going to be mended at the weekend. Promise me, that whatever happens, you will NOT climb through that hole in the fence."

"Promise," said Kung Fu Katy.

"Honest," said the boys.

"Off you go then," said Mrs Peep, and they jumped down from the table and ran into the garden to play.

"Have you got any toys?" said Hughie.

"Yes, I've got lots," said Kung Fu Katy.

"What toys have you got?" said Henry.

"Well, let's see now," said Katy, feeling so much happier now that the boys wanted to play.

"I've got bats and balls and bears and dolls, snakes and ladders and marbles and trolls, Ludo and Lego and tiddlywinks, some licking and sticking and fiddly things, a duck that waddles, a cuddly Fuzzle, scribbly scrabble and muddly puzzles, skittles and whistles and stacks and packs of cards and tricks and bricks and jacks. I've got dot to dot and bubbles for blowing, some string, a swing and things for sewing, a heap of books on kung fu by my bed and a cow that goes 'Mooooo' when you tread on its head."

"They're boring toys," said Henry.

"They're snoring toys," said Hughie.

"Well, let's play hide and seek then," said Kung Fu Katy.

"You two hide and then I'll come and find you.

But remember what my mum said, whatever happens, you must NOT climb through the hole in the fence."

"Come on then, Henry," said Hughie. "I've got a great place
to hide. Somewhere where she'll never ever find us in a
million billion years!"
Kung Fu Katy covered her eyes, and
counted to ten,
while the Horrors ran off to hide.

Well, she searched everywhere, absolutely everywhere.

Up and down the garden and behind the shed...

Nope.

Under the bushes and behind the trees...

Nope.

Inside the dustbin and outside the gate...

Nope.

Up the pipes, down the drains and in and out the hedge...

Nope,

nope,

nope.

Then, suddenly, she heard something move...

something at the bottom of the garden, just by the hole in the fence.

"OH NO!" cried Kung Fu Katy dashing to the bottom of the garden. "OH NO!!"

And as she poked her head through the hole in the fence she gasped in shock at the sight she saw.

For as her eyes peered all the way down a steep slithery slimy bank that slipped and slid into a trickling brook, that rippled and rolled into a swirling stream, she saw two tiny heads being swept away into a great gushing thunderous, rumbling, tumbling river.

"HELP! HELP! HELP!" they screamed,
"WE'VE FALLEN IN! WE CAN'T SWIM! SAVE US!
SAVE US! HELP! HELP! HELP!"

Without an extra second to lose,

Katy kicked off her shoes, and as quick as two flickers, she

yanked up her sleeves, stuffed her skirt in her knickers,

and with fisted fingers tightly clenched, she WHACKED

down a plank of wood from the fence.

BANG! BLAST! CHOP! CHOP! CHOP! Kung Fu Katy

couldn't stop.

She charged right down the bank, and lying on the plank on

her tummy wooshed into the brook,

swooshed into the stream,

and plunged into the rumbling, tumbling, roaring river.

"HANG ON BOYS!" she cried. "I'M COMING TO SAVE

YOU!"

Balancing on top of the sploshing torrents with sweat
gushing everywhere, she ripped off her frilliest
petticoat and hurled the lacy line into the water,
lassooing the boys together.

"HOLD TIGHT HORRORS! HOLD TIGHT! HOLD TIGHT!"
And with more power in her tiny body than Mr Universe,
Kung Fu Katy heaved those spluttering boys out of the
water and strapped them safely on to her back.

"KEEEEEEEE-YOWWWWWWWW!!!"
Then using her arms as oars, she ploughed them back
through the roaring river,
up the stream,
into the brook,
and hurled them back onto the bank to safety.

Woooooooooooooooooooooooooooshhh. PLOP!

Well, Hughie and Henry Horror slumped on to the grass like two great soggy sacks of potatoes, all tangled together in a sloshy fat heap.

"Oh, Katy!" howled Henry. "You saved our lives!"

"Oh, Katy!" sobbed Hughie. "You're the bravest and best cousin that anyone could ever wish for."

"Please, please forgive us," begged Henry.

Kung Fu Katy wiped her dripping hair off her face and looked down sadly at her muddy toes and scruffy dress.

"Oh dear," she sighed. "Just look at the state of me. My handbag's a wreck, my pearls have all popped off into the river, and my brand new dress and petticoats have ripped and torn into a thousand shreds."

"Well, I think you look fine," said Henry.

"Me too," agreed Hughie.

"Oh, please can we still stay with you?" whispered Henry in a tiny anxious voice.

Katy looked up at Hughie and Henry and her face
suddenly broke into a huge and happy grin.
"Maybe they're not such horrors after all!" she thought.
And they all walked arm-in-arm-in-arm through the fence
and back into the garden to play.